MR. MEN
MAGICAL
TREASURY

Roger Hargreaves

Original concept by
Roger Hargreaves

Written and Illustrated by
Adam Hargreaves

EGMONT

CONTENTS

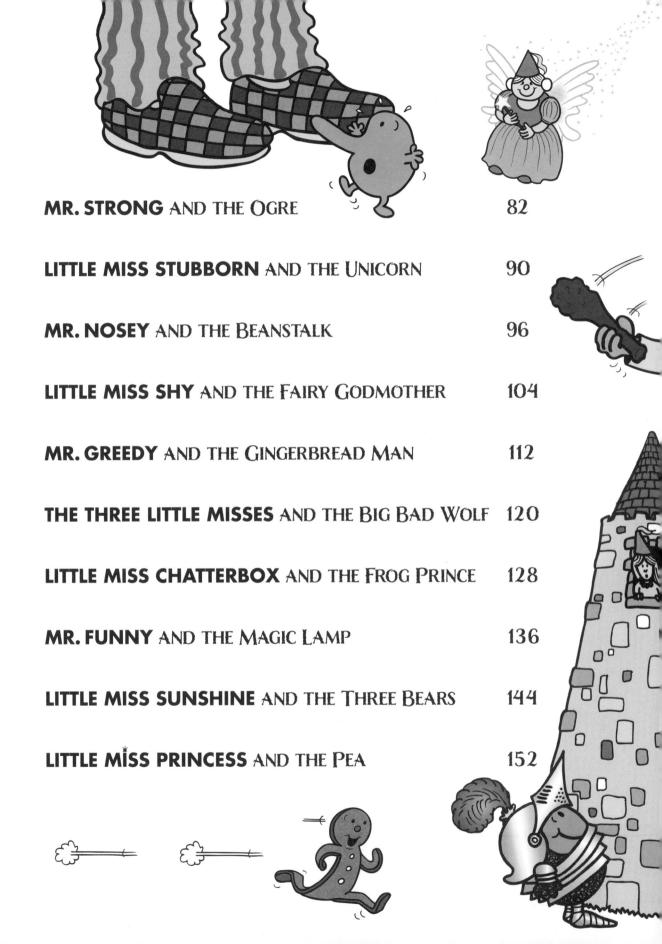

MR. HAPPY
AND THE WIZARD

Mr Happy goes to the Town Library every Saturday morning.

He went there last Saturday.

And he went there this Saturday.

He was looking along the shelves for a book to read when a very large and rather battered red volume caught his eye.

He pulled it out and looked at the spine.

It read, **'SPELL BOOK'**.

He was about to return it to its place when a voice suddenly said, "Don't you dare! I've been stuck on that shelf for a week!"

Mr Happy dropped the book in surprise.

"Ow!" said the book, for it was the book that had spoken.

There was a face on the cover – nose, eyes, mouth, everything!

Mr Happy was too amazed to speak.

"Oooh," wheezed the book. "You get terribly cramped if you're wedged on a shelf for too long. Now then, what's your name?"

"Mr Happy," said Mr Happy, finding his voice at last.

"Hello, I'm a spell book," said the book. "I belong to a Wizard, but the silly, absent-minded fool left me here. Look! He even forgot his hat! When I was asleep someone tidied me away up on that shelf. I need a lift home. Will you help me?"

Mr Happy agreed, and wearing the Wizard's hat, with the spell book under his arm, he set off through the countryside.

Mr Happy felt just like a real Wizard!

Along the way they met Mr Forgetful who was standing beside a phone box muttering to himself.

"Do you have any spells in there that could help Mr Forgetful's memory?" Mr Happy asked the spell book.

"Of course," said the spell book, and opened on the right page.

Mr Happy read out the spell and watched Mr Forgetful.

"I remember!" cried Mr Forgetful. "I've got to ring Mr Chatterbox … and I forgot to lock my house … oh no, I forgot to turn off my bath … and I didn't post that letter … and I haven't bought any milk … and I must water the plants and …"

Mr Forgetful was frantically running around in circles by this point, worrying about all the things he had forgotten.

"Oh dear! Do you have any spells to make people forget things?" Mr Happy said to the book.

The spell book opened at a different page and as soon as Mr Happy said the spell, Mr Forgetful looked a lot happier.

Mr Happy and the spell book continued on their way.

They heard somebody talking to himself around a bend in the road.

"If I cross over now then I might get run over, but if I don't cross over then how will I get to the other side? Oh dear, oh dear."

It was Mr Worry.

Mr Happy looked down at the spell book.

"Do you want to know if I have any spells to stop people worrying?" guessed the spell book, and opened to the right page.

Mr Happy read out the spell.

"I don't care!" shouted Mr Worry, suddenly. **"Hee! Hee!** I'm worry free! I'll just close my eyes and step out into the …"

CRASH! He walked straight into Mr Bump on his bicycle.

"Maybe worrying is safer after all," said Mr Happy, and the spell book flicked over a couple of pages to the spell that would return Mr Worry to normal.

It was a very long walk to the Wizard's house. In the middle of the afternoon Mr Happy caught up with a hot and tired Mr Small.

"How about a spell for longer legs?" suggested Mr Happy.

"Coming right up," replied the spell book.

Mr Small's legs grew and grew.

He strode off down the road at a terrific pace, until he reached a tree and banged his head on a branch. The same thing happened on the second tree he came to. And on the trees all the way down the road.

BANG!

OUCH!

BANG!

OUCH!

BANG!

OUCH!

Mr Happy winced.

"Shorter legs?" asked the spell book.

Mr Happy nodded.

By the evening they came to a wood.

"We're nearly there now," said the spell book happily.

Finally they reached a cottage in a clearing.

The Wizard opened the door. He was overjoyed.

"My spell book and my hat! I've been looking high and low for them for so long that I'd nearly given up hope! Thank you!"

He invited Mr Happy in for supper.

A Wizard's supper.

They ate **Everything Pie.**

The pie changed as they ate, so every mouthful tasted different!

After supper was finished and the washing-up spell had done its work, the Wizard turned to Mr Happy.

"There must be something I can do for you. Choose any spell you wish. Choose anything you want!"

Mr Happy smiled. "After seeing what spells can do, I think **I'm happy as I am!"** he laughed.

LITTLE MISS SUNSHINE
AND THE WICKED
WITCH

Little Miss Sunshine was going for a walk.

The weather was not very nice, but it takes a lot more than a bit of rain to dampen Little Miss Sunshine's spirits.

In the distance, she saw Little Miss Bossy approaching.

"I will be nice to Little Miss Bossy," thought Little Miss Sunshine, "so she won't boss me around."

However, as she got closer, the most incredible thing happened. There was a bright flash and Little Miss Bossy turned into **a bat!**

A blue, very squeaky, bossy sort of a bat.

"How extraordinary!" exclaimed Little Miss Sunshine, as she watched Little Miss Bossy flap her wings and fly away.

But almost as extraordinary, was the cackling laugh Little Miss Sunshine thought she heard coming from the clouds above.

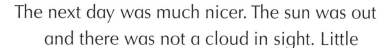

The next day was much nicer. The sun was out and there was not a cloud in sight. Little Miss Sunshine was happily walking along, wondering what had happened to Little Miss Bossy, when she saw Mr Rude walking towards her.

"I will be nice to Mr Rude," thought Little Miss Sunshine, "or he will be rude to me."

But at that moment there was a **bright flash.**
And when Little Miss Sunshine reached where
Mr Rude had been standing, she discovered
that he had turned into a toad.

A red, very rude, angry looking toad.

And just like the day before, Little Miss
Sunshine heard a
cackling laugh.
But this time it
seemed to be coming
from a nearby tree.

On her walk the following day,
Little Miss Sunshine had nearly caught
up with Little Miss Dotty when there was
another blinding flash.

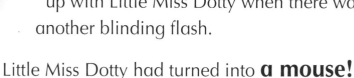

Little Miss Dotty had turned into **a mouse!**

A very confused, dotty, blond-haired mouse.

When Little Miss Sunshine heard the same
laugh she had heard the two days before,
she ducked behind a bush and waited to
see if she could find out who it came from.

Suddenly, with a rustle of leaves, a Witch
flew out from behind a tree.

14

A **Wicked Witch** on a **broomstick!**

A horrible hook-nosed, hairy, warty Wicked Witch, dressed in black.

Little Miss Sunshine felt very afraid, but she bravely decided to follow the Wicked Witch into Whispering Wood. It didn't take Little Miss Sunshine long to find the Wicked Witch's ramshackle cottage.

Nervously, Little Miss Sunshine crept up to the window and cautiously peered in.

The Wicked Witch was standing beside a large, black cauldron hanging over a fire. She was muttering to herself as she stirred revolting ingredients into the steaming pot. Little Miss Sunshine listened hard to hear what she was saying.

And this is what she heard:

"Hubble, bubble,
Toil and trouble,
Eye of newt and hair of hog,
Early tomorrow morning,
Turn Little Miss Sunshine into a dog!"

Little Miss Sunshine realised that **she needed help** and she needed it fast.

She tip-toed round to the front door where the Wicked Witch had left her broomstick leaning against the wall. And without thinking whether she could fly a broomstick or not, Little Miss Sunshine hopped on.

As it turned out she could. Just about. The broomstick rose up into the air with a **wobbly** Little Miss Sunshine perched on top.

Little Miss Sunshine knew exactly who would be able to help - Little Miss Magic. The broomstick took her to Little Miss Magic's house in no time at all.

"There's a Wicked Witch living in Whispering Wood,"

explained Little Miss Sunshine, breathlessly, when she arrived. She then told Little Miss Magic what she had seen and more importantly what she had heard.

"... and I'm going to be turned into a dog tomorrow morning!" she gasped.

"That's awful!" said Little Miss Magic. "But this is just the sort of problem that I like dealing with."

"I hoped you would say that," said Little Miss Sunshine.

"Now, I'll tell you what we are going to do ..." continued Little Miss Magic.

The next day, at sunrise, Little Miss Sunshine and Little Miss Magic knocked at the Wicked Witch's door.

The Wicked Witch opened it and with a flash, her spell turned Little Miss Sunshine into a **dog.**

"Hee, hee, hee," cackled the Wicked Witch. "That worked like a dream."

It was then that Little Miss Magic turned the Wicked Witch into a cat!

A smelly, scraggy, black cat.

A smelly, scraggy, black cat that suddenly found herself looking up at a scary yellow dog.

The Wicked Witch cat let out a screech and fled.

And, barking noisily, the Little Miss Sunshine dog set off in pursuit and chased the Wicked Witch cat far away. So far away that she would never find her way back.

When Little Miss Sunshine returned, Little Miss Magic turned her back into her old self. She then found Little Miss Bossy and Mr Rude and turned them back to normal as well.

Little Miss Dotty took a lot longer to find as she was hidden in a mouse hole, and being the dotty person that she is, she seemed not to have noticed that anything had happened.

"Are you feeling all right?" asked Little Miss Sunshine, after Little Miss Magic had said a few magic words.

"Why, of course I am," said Little Miss Dotty. "Why shouldn't I?"

"Oh, no reason," said Little Miss Sunshine, winking at Little Miss Magic.

"Although," said Little Miss Dotty, twitching her nose, "I really fancy a nice piece of ..."

"... cheese!"

MR. TICKLE
AND THE DRAGON

Mr Tickle was having a very good day. Twenty one people well and truly tickled. A very good day indeed.

But when he arrived home, he could not believe his eyes.

"I can't believe my eyes," he said to himself. "Somebody has burnt down my house!"

Mr Tickle's house was gone. All that was left was a smoking, charred pile at the end of his garden path.

There was more smoke rising from the end of the lane.

Mr Tickle set off to investigate.

The smoke was coming from Mr Funny's shoe car. Or rather, it had been his car, but all that remained was a burnt shoelace.

Mr Tickle could see another spiral of smoke in the distance.

This time it was Mr Clever's house, and very nearly Mr Clever by the look of him!

"I just got out in time," said Mr Clever. "There can only be one culprit. It must have been a ..."

But Mr Tickle did not wait to hear what it must have been. He had spotted the signs of another fire and was determined to follow the trail.

It was a long trail which led from Mr Chatterbox's burnt out phone box to Farmer Field's burnt down barn, and on through wilder, bleaker land, up into the mountains. Soon it began to get dark, but Mr Tickle continued to climb higher and higher.

Darkness had fallen when he saw a bright light. In the distance, there was a cave emitting a red glow.

Suddenly Mr Tickle did not feel very brave. Suddenly he wished he had stayed to hear what Mr Clever had to say.

Mr Tickle decided to wait there until the morning. He curled up under a bush and wrapped his arms around himself three times to keep warm.

Mr Tickle fell into a surprisingly deep sleep and the sun was up when he was woken by the rustling of the bush.

Mr Tickle opened an eye.

The bush rustled again.

"I know you're in there," rumbled a very deep voice. **"Come on! Show yourself!"**

Mr Tickle cautiously poked his head through the top of the bush and stood blinking in the bright sunlight. He was quite unprepared for the sight that met his eyes.

He was standing face to face with **a dragon!**

A huge dragon at that. A huge dragon with smoke curling from his nostrils.

Mr Tickle gulped.

"Hello," said Mr Tickle, in a tiny voice.

"I'm going to give you thirty seconds to give me a good reason why I shouldn't burn you to a crisp," bellowed the dragon, **"and then I'm going to burn you to a crisp!"**

Mr Tickle gulped for the second time.

Mr Tickle needed to think fast. He realised his arms were hidden. Quick as a flash he sent one of his extraordinarily long arms snaking through the bushes and under the Dragon's belly.

Mr Tickle flexed his fingers and hoped beyond everything that dragons are ticklish.

The Dragon instantly crumbled into a giggling, laughing tangle on the ground.

"Ha! **Ha!** Ha!" roared the Dragon.

"**Hee!** Hee! Hee!" wheezed the Dragon.

"Ho! Ho! **Ho!**" boomed the Dragon.

"Stop it! Stop it!" he cried.

"I'll stop tickling if you promise to stop burning things," said Mr Tickle.

"**Anything! I'll promise anything!**" pleaded the Dragon.

Mr Tickle stopped tickling and looked the Dragon squarely in the eye.

"What you need to learn," said Mr Tickle, "is to put your fire breathing to good use. You should be using your extraordinary skills to make people happy. I'll show you."

24

The Dragon lay down on the ground and Mr Tickle hopped on his back. Then the Dragon shook out his great wings and took off, circling high over the mountains and swooping down to the distant valleys.

They flew lower and lower, passing over barns and cottages.

"Look!" cried Mr Tickle. "It's Little Miss Splendid's house. I have an idea for your first good deed!"

Mr Tickle and the Dragon stood beside Little Miss Splendid's swimming pool.

"It is too cold today to swim in Little Miss Splendid's pool," said Mr Tickle. "Do you think you could do anything about that?"

The Dragon thought for a moment.

Then he took a deep breath and breathed out through his nostrils. Flames licked across the surface of the swimming pool. In no time at all the pool was steaming.

Little Miss Splendid was delighted. Mr Tickle, the Dragon and Little Miss Splendid had a very enjoyable swim.

In fact, the Dragon had a very enjoyable day.

He melted the ice on Mr Bump's path, and Mr Bump couldn't have been happier, as most mornings he usually slipped up and bumped his head.

He warmed up Mr Forgetful's cup of tea which he had made at breakfast time and forgotten to drink. Mr Forgetful was delighted. He doesn't normally get to drink hot tea!

And Mr Greedy was very impressed when the Dragon cooked fifteen sausages all at once.

By the end of the day, the Dragon had a big glowing smile across his face.

"Do you know what?" he boomed, cheerfully. **"I feel really good!"**

Mr Tickle grinned and then he reached out his extraordinarily long arms ... and tickled the Dragon!

"And now I do too!" he laughed.

LITTLE MISS NAUGHTY
AND THE GOOD
FAIRY

Little Miss Naughty got up, stretched, opened her curtains and looked out of her window.

"What's that?" she said, peering more closely.

She went downstairs, out of the back door and down to the bottom of her garden.

"Look at that!" she cried. "It's a **Fairy ring!**"

On the ground at her feet was a ring of mushrooms growing in the dewy grass.

"I wonder what happens if I step into the ring?" thought Little Miss Naughty out loud.

So she did.

And what happened was that she shrank to the size of a matchbox.

Which surprised her enormously.

"Oh help!" she wailed. "What do I do now?"

She looked around the Fairy ring and noticed that there was a door in the stem of one of the mushrooms.

"I wonder what happens if I go through that door?" she asked herself.

So she did.

And what happened was that she found herself in a quite different world.

Fairyland!

Little Miss Naughty stepped out into a beautiful, magical wood. On a hilltop in the distance was a glittering castle. Little Miss Naughty set off to see who lived there.

"Who are you?" asked a voice above her.

Startled, Little Miss Naughty looked up to find a Fairy with gossamer wings hovering just above her head.

"I'm Little Miss Good," lied Little Miss Naughty.

"What a coincidence! I'm the Good Fairy. You must come and stay the night."

The Good Fairy waved her magic wand and whisked them up to her castle.

And it was the Good Fairy's magic wand that captured Little Miss Naughty's attention all evening long.

Little Miss Naughty could think of nothing but the mischief she might get up to if she was a Fairy with her own magic wand and her own wings.

That night Little Miss Naughty was **very naughty.**

She stole the Good Fairy's wand!

She crept out of the castle and ran all the way back to the magical wood where she had entered Fairyland. There she found a door in a tree which opened into the ring of mushrooms at the bottom of her garden.

As soon as she stepped out of the Fairy ring she grew back to her normal size.

Once Little Miss Naughty was safely inside her house she looked at the wand in her trembling hand.

She closed her eyes and waved the wand and at the same time she said, **"Turn me into a Fairy."**

When she opened her eyes and looked in the mirror she saw she had a perfect pair of Fairy wings.

She gave them a little flutter and felt herself rise off the floor.

"Oh what fun!" she cried. "Oh, what fun I am going to have!"

The next day, flying along above the rooftops she saw Mr Bump walking along the pavement.

She waved the magic wand and a hole appeared in front of Mr Bump and in he fell.

From her perch on a chimney pot high above, Little Miss Naughty chuckled to herself.

But at that very moment a high wall fell across the pavement just where Mr Bump would have been walking if he hadn't fallen into the hole.

"Thank goodness I fell into this hole," said Mr Bump, peering up the street.

Little Miss Naughty flew out across the countryside where she found Farmer Barns looking at his field of corn.

With another **chuckle,** Little Miss Naughty waved the wand and the field of corn turned into a ploughed field.

But there in the middle of the field was the farmer's dog who had been lost amongst the corn.

"Thank goodness the corn disappeared and I have found Fido," said a relieved Farmer Barns.

Little Miss Naughty was very **puzzled.**

It seemed that as hard as she tried to be naughty, things kept turning out for the best.

She made it rain on Little Miss Sunshine, who could not have been happier because her tomatoes needed watering.

She created a mess in Little Miss Neat's front room and Little Miss Neat was overjoyed because she had Mr Messy coming for tea later that day and she wanted to make him feel at home.

By the time Little Miss Naughty got home she had never caused so much happiness in her life.

She was miserable.

"This thing's no good," she said, throwing the wand down on the table.

"That is where you are very wrong," said a voice.

Little Miss Naughty nearly jumped out of her skin.

It was the Good Fairy.

"That wand is all good because it is my wand. I hope that making so many people happy may have done **you** some good."

"So this wand will only make good things happen?" asked Little Miss Naughty.

"That's right."

"And this wand will never allow you to do anything naughty?"

"That's right."

"There is one more thing I need to know," said Little Miss Naughty.

"What is that?" asked the Good Fairy.

"Where does the Naughty Fairy live?"

MR. JELLY
AND THE PIRATES

Mr Jelly is the most nervous person you will ever meet. The slightest thing will send him into a panic.

Even the sound of the wind in the trees will make him bolt behind the sofa, quivering and shaking in fear.

So as you can imagine, it takes Mr Jelly a long time to pluck up enough courage to go on holiday.

This year, Mr Jelly went to Seatown.

Mr Jelly longed to join everyone playing in the sea, but he was too frightened.

"Why don't you go for a swim?" suggested Mr Lazy.

"I ... I'm too scared," admitted Mr Jelly. "There might be nasty seaweed ... or a crab ... or ... or a **shark!"**

"Well, why don't you go out in my dinghy?" replied Mr Lazy.

"I ... I ... might drift out to sea and never be found again," said Mr Jelly, trembling at the thought.

"No you won't," said Mr Lazy. "Not if I hold on to the rope."

Mr Jelly thought this over and decided to risk it.

After a while, Mr Jelly began to enjoy himself in the dinghy. But when he looked back, he discovered that he was a very long way from the beach. Mr Lazy had fallen asleep and the rope had slipped through his fingers!

"Oh help! Oh help! A wave is going to turn over the boat and I'm going to be swallowed by a whale!" shrieked Mr Jelly. But he was too far away for anyone to hear him.

Before long the land disappeared and large, black storm clouds gathered on the horizon.

Thunder **boomed** and lightning **crackled.** The sea rose up in a great roaring mass that tossed the little dinghy from wave to wave.

Mr Jelly cowered in the bottom of the boat.

"Oh help! Oh help! he shrieked. "I'm going to be struck by lightning, and burnt to a crisp, and tipped out of the boat and drowned!"

And then he fainted.

When he came to, he discovered that he had been washed up onto a tiny, deserted island.

Mr Jelly stared out at the vast expanse of sea.

"Oh help," he said in a very small voice, and then he fainted again.

Mr Jelly was woken by the sound of digging. He peered through the bushes at the side of the beach. What he saw filled him with terror...

Three swashbuckling, **ruthless-looking pirates** were digging up a treasure chest!

Mr Jelly knew that he must not make a sound, but the more he tried not to make a sound, the more he wobbled and trembled in fear. And the more he wobbled and trembled, the more the bushes shook and rustled.

So, in a very short time, Mr Jelly was found and set, quivering, on the sand in front of the pirates.

"Well, shiver my timbers, if he ain't just what we need," growled the pirate Captain. **"A cabin boy!"**

The three pirates and their new cabin boy rowed out to their ship, anchored in the bay.

Mr Jelly shook and trembled and quivered in terror.

The pirates, who prided themselves on their bravery, chuckled and laughed. They had never met anyone as nervous as Mr Jelly.

And over the following week, they came to realise just how nervous Mr Jelly really was.

On the first day, the first mate ordered Mr Jelly up into the rigging to set the sail.

"Oh help! Oh help!"

shrieked Mr Jelly. "It's so high up and I'm going to have to climb and climb, and then I'll be even higher up, and I'll get dizzy, and I'll fall down into the sea and I'll be eaten by a shark!"

And then he fainted.

Luckily he had only climbed two rungs and the first mate caught him easily.

"I'd never thought of that," murmured the first mate to himself.

The next day, the quartermaster ordered Mr Jelly to sharpen the cutlasses on the grinding stone.

"Oh help! Oh help!" shrieked Mr Jelly. "I'll make the cutlass very sharp, and it will be so sharp that I will cut my finger, and then I'll bleed and bleed and ..."

And then he fainted.

"I'd never thought of that," mumbled the quartermaster to himself.

On the third day, the gunner ordered Mr Jelly to practise firing the cannon.

"Oh help! Oh help!" shrieked Mr Jelly. "I'll load the cannon, and then fire the cannon and the explosion will be so loud that I'll go deaf, and then I won't be able to hear anything, and then ..."

And then ... well, you know what happened then.

He fainted.

Again.

"I'd never thought of that," muttered the gunner to himself.

And so it continued all week.

Mr Jelly even fainted when the cook ordered him to light the stove in the galley because he was afraid he would set the ship on fire!

41

And a very strange thing happened during the week. Not only did the pirates discover how nervous Mr Jelly was, but they also began to find out how nervous they were, too.

The more Mr Jelly shrieked and fainted and quivered and quaked at what terrible accidents might happen, the more the pirates found themselves worrying. By the end of the week, the pirate Captain found himself with a crew who were too scared to do anything.

Even the ship's carpenter had downed tools because he was afraid he might get a splinter!

"This is hopeless!" roared the Captain. "How can we call ourselves pirates? That cabin boy has turned you all into scaredy cats. Mr Jelly must walk the plank!"

So, Mr Jelly was pushed out onto the plank.

"Oh help! Oh help!" shrieked Mr Jelly. "Don't make me walk the plank. I'll fall into the sea and then I'll have to swim for hours and hours and then I'll get weaker and weaker and then I'll drown!"

"That's horrible," said the first mate.

"Yeh, really nasty," agreed the quartermaster.

"We can't do that," said the gunner.

And the rest of the crew agreed.

"That's it!" cried the Captain. "I give up. Do what you want!"

And the crew did.

They sailed, very cautiously and very slowly, to Seatown, where they let Mr Jelly off.

Mr Jelly found Mr Lazy on the beach.

Fast asleep.

Mr Lazy yawned, stretched and opened an eye. "Hello," he said, sleepily. "Did you have fun? Sorry I fell asleep, but here you are safe and sound."

Mr Jelly began to **wobble** and **quiver** and **shake.**

But not in fear.

Mr Jelly was **very, very, very angry!**

LITTLE MISS TROUBLE AND THE MERMAID

The trouble with Little Miss Trouble is that she is always causing trouble.

Like when she met Mr Greedy.

"Do you know that they are giving away ice-creams around the corner?" she asked him.

"Really!" cried Mr Greedy, and raced off to get some.

What he did not know, and Little Miss Trouble did, was that workmen had dug up the pavement around the corner.

Mr Greedy fell right down the hole. **THUMP!**

Little Miss Trouble thought this was very funny.

Mr Greedy did not.

Now, the trouble with making trouble is that sometimes it can catch up with you.

And that is what happened when Little Miss Trouble went to Seatown last week.

Her first two days in Seatown were **great fun.** Great fun for her, but **no fun** for anybody else!

She splashed Little Miss Splendid, and blamed Little Miss Chatterbox.

Who Little Miss Splendid sprayed with cold seawater!

Little Miss Trouble kicked sand all over Mr Strong and then blamed Mr Sneeze.

Who Mr Strong buried in sand up to his nose!

Little Miss Trouble was having the time of her life. She had never caused so much trouble!

On her third day in Seatown, she decided to go fishing with Mr Muddle and Little Miss Bossy. The three of them rowed out to sea and set up their fishing rods.

Little Miss Trouble was trying to think of the best way to cause trouble when she felt something tug on her fishing line.

"I've caught **a fish!"** she cried, excitedly.

Then there was another tug. A much stronger tug. A tug so strong that it pulled her right out of the boat!

Not only did it pull her out of the boat, it pulled her down into the sea.

Little Miss Trouble let go of the fishing line, but something, or someone, grabbed her foot and dragged her deeper and deeper.

It was not until she reached the bottom of the sea that she discovered who had caught her.

It was a mermaid!

"There is someone who wishes to see you," said the Mermaid to a flabbergasted Little Miss Trouble.

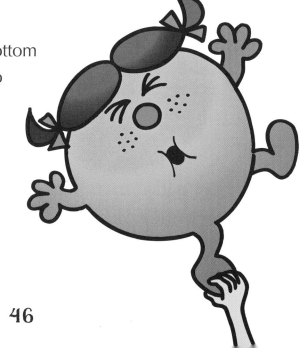

"Take me back!" demanded Little Miss Trouble.

"Later," said the Mermaid. "Now, follow me."

Little Miss Trouble realised that she had no choice in the matter, so she did as she was told.

The Mermaid took Little Miss Trouble's hand and led her across the seabed.

After a short while, they came to a coral reef.

"Where are you taking me?" asked Little Miss Trouble.

"You are about to find out," replied the Mermaid.

In the middle of the reef was a circle of sand and in the middle of the circle was a coral throne.

And sitting on the throne was the **Mermaid Queen.**

"I have brought Little Miss Trouble as you ordered, Your Highness," said the Mermaid.

"So **you** are the person who has been causing so much **trouble** on my beach and in my sea!" said the Mermaid Queen, angrily. "It is time that you learnt to behave yourself. No more splashing people and kicking sand around."

"But it wasn't me!" exclaimed Little Miss Trouble. "It was Little Miss Chatterbox and Mr ..."

To Little Miss Trouble's huge surprise, the word **'sneeze',** which she had meant to say, came out as a **bubble.**

And every time she tried to say it, the same thing happened, until there was a stream of bubbles coming out of her mouth!

"It is no good you blaming other people and getting them into trouble," said the Mermaid Queen. "From now on, every time you try to make trouble, all that you will get for your trouble is bubbles! You may go back to the beach now."

The Mermaid led Little Miss Trouble away. They swam to the edge of the coral reef, where a dolphin was waiting.

"This dolphin will take you back to Seatown. **Do not forget** what the Queen said," warned the Mermaid.

Little Miss Trouble held on to the dolphin's fin and rode her back to the beach, where the dolphin left her at the shore.

The beach was crowded and as Little Miss Trouble watched the dolphin's fin as it swam away, an idea struck her.

"There's a … !" she shouted, at the top of her voice, but instead of the word **'shark',** which she had meant to shout to scare everyone, a huge **bubble** came out of her mouth.

And then another.

Everyone on the beach gave her a very odd look.

Feeling very foolish, Little Miss Trouble went back to her hotel.

The next morning, she felt much better.

Down on the beach, she found Little Miss Sunshine sunbathing on a beach towel. Little Miss Trouble crept up behind her and dropped her ice-cream on to Little Miss Sunshine!

"What was that?" screamed Little Miss Sunshine, leaping up in surprise. **"Who did that?"**

"It was …" began Little Miss Trouble.

She was about to say, 'Mr Rush', but I am sure you know what came out instead.

That's right!

An enormous **bubble!**

And then **more** and **more** and **more** bubbles.

And that was not all.

"How could you!" cried Little Miss Sunshine, and she threw what was left of the ice-cream at Little Miss Trouble.

There was nothing Little Miss Trouble could say.

Because she could not speak.

All she could do was blow **bubbles.**

And so it went on.

Every time Little Miss Trouble tried to cause trouble, the same thing happened.

By the end of the week, Little Miss Trouble had given up trying to make trouble and had started building sandcastles instead.

In fact, she became so good at building sandcastles that she **won the sandcastle competition!** She was very excited, until she discovered what the prize was.

A year's supply of **bubble bath!**

MR. BUMP
AND THE KNIGHT

Mr Bump was thoroughly fed up. It did not seem to matter what he did, he always ended up getting bumped and bruised or scraped and scratched.

So, you can imagine how hard it was for him to find a job.

He had tried working at the baker's, but he had burnt his fingers on the bread oven.

OUCH!

He had tried being a bricklayer, but he had dropped a brick on his foot.

THUD!

OUCH!

He had even tried working at the pillow factory.

Who could hurt themselves in a pillow factory?

Mr Bump, of course!

He got a feather in his eye!

OUCH!

Every day it was bandage this and bandage that.

Poor Mr Bump was very fed up.

Then one day, while Mr Bump was walking in the woods behind his house, he met someone who gave him a wonderful idea.

The perfect idea for a new job.

That someone was a Knight in shining armour, riding by on his horse.

Now, it was not the thought of the excitement and adventure of being a Knight that caught Mr Bump's imagination, nor was it the idea of the fame and fortune he might win. No, it was the Knight's solid, metal armour that caught his eye.

Shining armour that protected the Knight from **bumps** and bruises, scrapes and scratches.

"If I wore armour like that," thought Mr Bump to himself, "I would never need to worry about bumping myself again. I shall become **a Knight.**"

Early the next morning, Mr Bump rushed to the blacksmith's to buy himself a suit of armour.

The blacksmith had to put the armour on very carefully to avoid Mr Bump's bruises, but when he had it on, Mr Bump looked at his reflection in the mirror and smiled.

Mr Bump then bought a book called *'Knights, All You Need to Know'*.

"Now," said Mr Bump, opening the book, "what do Knights do?"

He read a whole chapter about jousting. Then he went out and bought a horse and a lance and went to a local jousting tournament.

However, Mr Bump quickly found out that he was not very good at jousting. Every time he sat on his horse he fell off.

CRASH!

The other Knights thought it was hilarious.

That evening, Mr Bump opened his book and read a chapter called 'Saving Damsels in Distress'.

The next day, he set off, on foot, to find a damsel in need of saving.

Fortunately, because it was very awkward walking in a suit of armour, Mr Bump found one near his house.

A damsel locked in a very tall tower.

"Will you save me, Sir Knight?" cried the Damsel.

"I will!" Mr Bump called back.

The Damsel let down a ladder woven from her long, fine hair.

But try as hard as he might, Mr Bump could not climb the ladder.

He kept falling off at every attempt.

BANG! CRASH! CLUNK!

Feeling rather sorry for himself, and even more sorry for the Damsel, Mr Bump trudged off home.

The next chapter in the book was entitled **'Slaying Dragons'.**

"That's the one for me!" cried Mr Bump.

The following day, Mr Bump
bought a sword and shield and
went in search of a dragon.
There were not any nearby,
so he caught the bus.

The dragon was asleep on the
top of a steep hill.

It took Mr Bump a lot of
huffing and puffing to climb to the top.

When he finally reached the top, he raised his sword above his
head to slay the dragon, but the weight of the sword tipped
Mr Bump off balance.

With a great

CRASHING

and

CLATTERING

of armour, he rolled all the way down the hill.

It was a **very sad** Mr Bump who got back home later that day.

He had to face the fact that he was not cut out to be a Knight.

He went up to his bedroom and took off his armour.

And then he noticed something **quite remarkable.**

When he glimpsed himself in the mirror, it was a very different Mr Bump looking back at him.

A Mr Bump without a bandage or a plaster in sight.

A Mr Bump without a bump or a bruise.

Mr Bump **smiled.**

And then he **laughed …**

… and then he fell over backwards and **bumped his head on the bed!**

LITTLE MISS SPLENDID AND THE PRINCESS

Little Miss Splendid, as her name suggests, is very splendid. She wears splendid hats and lives in a splendid house.

And how does Little Miss Splendid know she is so splendid?

She knows because she has a **magic mirror** that tells her so.

Each morning, Little Miss Splendid goes into her dressing room and stands in front of the mirror.

"Mirror, mirror, on the wall, who is the most splendid of all?" she asks the mirror.

"Little Miss Splendid is the most splendid of all," answers the mirror.

Next door to Little Miss Splendid's very splendid house is a castle, which has stood empty for many years.

One day, on her way to the shops, Little Miss Splendid noticed a sold sign on the castle gate.

"I wonder who has bought that?" she thought to herself.

The following day, she found out.

Little Miss Splendid was woken by a **fanfare** of trumpets. She looked out of the window to see three removal vans and a very splendid-looking coach and horses moving in procession up the castle drive.

A **Princess** had moved in next door!

At first, Little Miss Splendid was very excited.

"Living next door to a Princess must make me even more splendid," she told herself, as she walked to her dressing room.

She put on her most splendid hat and got ready to visit her new next-door neighbour. But, before she left, she stood before her magic mirror.

"Mirror, mirror, on the wall, who is the most splendid of all?" she asked the mirror.

"The **Princess** next door is the most splendid of all," answered the mirror.

Little Miss Splendid could not believe her ears. "But **I'm** the most splendid of all!"

"Not any longer," pointed out the mirror.

Little Miss Splendid watched the Princess for the rest of that week.

She looked at the Princess's splendid coach. She studied the Princess's splendid crown. And she noted the Princess's splendid robe.

Everywhere she went nobody noticed her any longer. All they talked about was the Princess and how splendid she looked.

Little Miss Splendid grew more and more jealous of the Princess.

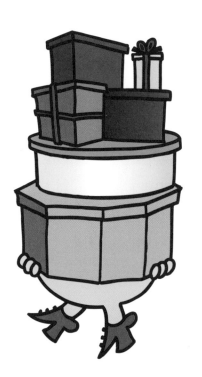

The following week, Little Miss Splendid went shopping. She bought an incredibly ornate coach and four horses, a shimmering princess's hat and a splendidly long and flowing robe.

Little Miss Splendid was so pleased with her new purchases that she went straight into town to show them off. But no one took any notice of her.

"Good morning, Miss Splendid," said Mr Happy, without any comment on what she was wearing. "Did you hear that the Princess is coming into town later? I can't wait, **it's so exciting!"**

A very disappointed Little Miss Splendid went home and looked in her magic mirror.

"I do look splendid," she told herself, admiring her reflection.

But the mirror disagreed.

"The Princess next door is the most splendid of all," said the mirror. "And if I may say, you look **a little ridiculous."**

Little Miss Splendid was dismayed. But, what could she do?

The next morning, the answer came to her when she was reading the newspaper. The Princess had placed an advertisement for a coachman, a maid and a butler.

Little Miss Splendid smiled to herself.

A little later, she went round to see Mr Bump.

"There is a job going as the Princess's coachman," she told Mr Bump. "It would be perfect for you."

"Really?" said Mr Bump, as he accidentally broke his window.

He hurried over to the castle to apply.

Then Little Miss Splendid went to see Little Miss Scatterbrain and suggested that she applied to be the Princess's maid.

"Really?" said Little Miss Scatterbrain, rushing off to the castle as fast as she could.

Lastly, Little Miss Splendid visited Mr Muddle who was very excited at the idea of being the Princess's butler – although he took a few wrong turns before he remembered how to get to the castle!

When Little Miss Splendid saw the Princess next, it was very obvious that her three friends had got the jobs.

Mr Bump had **crashed** the Princess's coach and **wrecked it.**

Little Miss Scatterbrain had **ironed** the Princess's robe and **burnt** a large hole in it.

And Mr Muddle had **muddled up** the crown and the bread. He had put the bread in the safe and the Princess's crown in the oven and **melted it!**

The Princess did not look in the least splendid.

Little Miss Splendid stood in front of her magic mirror.

"Mirror, mirror, on the wall, who is the most splendid of all?" she asked.

"Little Miss Splendid is the most splendid of all," came the reluctant reply.

"I knew I was the most splendid of all!" cried Little Miss Splendid.

"Although," continued the mirror …

… "I did hear that the **Queen** is coming to stay!"

MR. NOISY AND THE GIANT

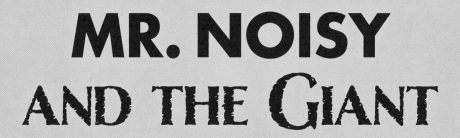

Mr Noisy is the **noisiest** person you will ever meet.

His voice is **so loud** it can shake the birds from the trees.

It can even shake the birds from the trees across the other side of the world!

Last month, Mr Noisy decided to call his friend Mr Quiet, who lives many, many hills away.

But Mr Noisy does not have a telephone. He does not need one.

Do you know what he does when he wants to speak to someone?

He goes out of his front door and **shouts!**

When Mr Quiet heard Mr Noisy's booming voice, he nearly jumped out of his chair.

Mr Noisy's **loud voice** scares most people.

When Mr Jelly met Mr Noisy, he was so frightened that he ran straight home and stayed under his bed for a week.

And when Mr Noisy said hello to Little Miss Splendid, he made her hair stand on end.

But Mr Noisy is not the only person with a **huge voice.**

There is one other person who is just as loud as Mr Noisy.

That person is a **Giant.**

A Giant who lives surprisingly close to where you live, but even closer to Mr Noisy.

The Giant is enormous.

His feet are the size of sofas.

He is so tall that he has to bend down to look into Mr Tall's bedroom window.

But by far the biggest thing about the Giant is his voice.

And that is the Giant's biggest problem in life.

Whenever he tries to talk to anyone, they run away.

His huge, loud, booming, thunderous voice terrifies everybody.

Just one **"HELLO!"** is enough to send them running for the hills.

And so the Giant is a very sad and lonely Giant.

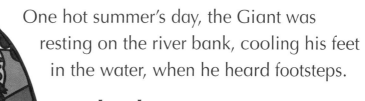

One hot summer's day, the Giant was resting on the river bank, cooling his feet in the water, when he heard footsteps.

Very **loud,** thumping footsteps.

And the very loud, thumping footsteps were accompanied by **whistling.**

Whistling as loudly as a train whistle.

The Giant was very excited.

That must be another Giant, he thought to himself.

Another Giant who could be my friend.

The Giant peered over the hill. But on the other side of the hill, he did not see another Giant.

I am sure you can guess who he saw instead.

That's right!

It was Mr Noisy!

"HELLO!" boomed the Giant, in his quietest voice.

But because Mr Noisy is so used to loud noises he did not run away like anyone else would have.

"HELLO!" he boomed back, in a voice as loud as the Giant's.

In no time at all, the Giant and Mr Noisy were chatting.

The **loudest** chat in the world!

The Giant so enjoyed their chat that he invited Mr Noisy to tea.

And to the Giant's delight, Mr Noisy accepted his invitation.

The Giant talked and talked and talked, while Mr Noisy sat sipping tea out of the Giant's thimble.

They talked right through the afternoon and into the evening.

They talked so late that Mr Noisy was invited to stay the night.

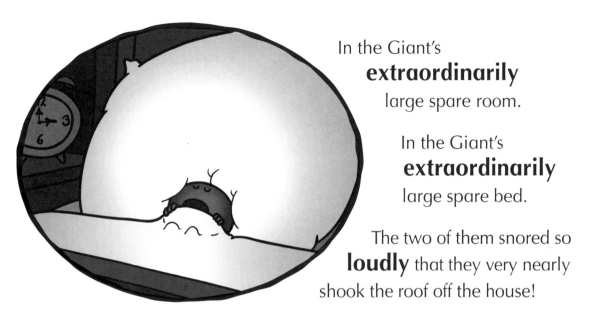

In the Giant's
extraordinarily
large spare room.

In the Giant's
extraordinarily
large spare bed.

The two of them snored so
loudly that they very nearly
shook the roof off the house!

The next morning, while having a swim in the Giant's extraordinarily large bath, Mr Noisy had an idea.

He explained his idea to the Giant over breakfast.

"I HAVE A FRIEND CALLED MR QUIET," boomed Mr Noisy, "AND HE USED TO LIVE IN A PLACE CALLED LOUDLAND. I THINK THAT YOU AND I SHOULD GO ON HOLIDAY TO LOUDLAND!"

"WHAT A GREAT IDEA!" thundered the Giant.

And so off they went.

And it was **perfect.**

Because, you see, in Loudland everything and everybody is loud.

Extremely loud.

Even the worms are loud in Loudland.

Mr Noisy and the Giant could be **as loud as they liked.**

They fitted in very well.

Except for one thing.

One very **LARGE** thing.

The Giant could not fit into his hotel bed!

LITTLE MISS LUCKY
AND THE NAUGHTY
PIXIES

Little Miss Lucky, as I am sure you know, is the luckiest person in the world.

When she goes out for a walk, she always finds a pound coin lying on the ground.

She never gets caught in the rain.

And even when things go wrong, she is lucky.

The other week she locked herself out of Horseshoe cottage, where she lives, and guess who should come round the corner?

Mr Latchkey the locksmith!

However, last week, strange things started to happen to Little Miss Lucky.

The sort of things that never normally happened to her.

Unlucky things.

She walked under a ladder and a pot of paint fell on her head.

SPLAT!

When she was walking down the high street, she fell into an open manhole.

BUMP!

And as she was passing someone's garden, she was soaked by a sprinkler.

SPLASH!

Little Miss Lucky could not understand what was going on.

But have you noticed anything? Have you noticed anyone new nearby when these unlucky things happen? That's right, some **small troublemakers** are playing tricks on her!

And do you know who they are?

I'll tell you.

They are Pixies. **Very naughty Pixies!**

Poor Little Miss Lucky did not know that Pixies were to blame though. She thought that her luck had run out.

She was so worried that she went to see Doctor Makeyouwell.

But the Doctor was not there. And nobody knew what had happened to him.

"More bad luck," thought Little Miss Lucky to herself.

The next day, she paid another visit to Doctor Makeyouwell's surgery.

But, again, he was not there.

Double bad luck!

On her way home, Little Miss Lucky met Little Miss Wise and explained to her how she had run out of luck.

"I suspect," suggested Little Miss Wise, "that it is not so much a case of bad luck, as somebody playing tricks on you. Somebody like Mr Mischief, for instance."

The more Little Miss Lucky thought this over, the more she hoped that Little Miss Wise was right.

That evening she devised a plan to **catch** the culprit.

She sprinkled flour on the floor round her bed before she went to sleep.

In the middle of the night, while Little Miss Lucky was fast asleep, those naughty Pixies crept into her house.

Their first **naughty** deed was to swap the sugar in the sugar bowl with the salt in the salt-cellar.

Then the Pixies **sneaked** upstairs and left the largest alarm clock you have ever seen on Little Miss Lucky's bedside table.

Very early the next morning, Little Miss Lucky was **rudely** awoken by the most awful noise.

**CLANG!
CLANG!
CLANG!**

rang the giant alarm clock.

Little Miss Lucky's ears were ringing.

When she looked down at the floor, there was a trail of floury footprints for her to follow out of the door and down the stairs.

Floury footprints that were much too small to be Mr Mischief's.

And, as I am sure you can guess, those floury footprints led Little Miss Lucky all the way to where the Pixies lived.

The Pixies were so surprised and worried at being caught that they promised there and then to never play another trick on Little Miss Lucky.

Little Miss Lucky left feeling very happy knowing that she was just as lucky as she had always been.

When she got home, she made herself a well-earned breakfast. Eggs on toast and a pot of tea.

She was so busy thinking about the Pixies that, without realising, Little Miss Lucky poured salt in her tea and sugar on her eggs!

But you and I know that she didn't, did she?!

Because of the naughty Pixies' night time tricks, her breakfast was not spoiled.

Now, that's what I call lucky!

MR. STRONG
AND THE OGRE

Mr Strong is the strongest person in the World. He is so strong he can balance an elephant on one finger.

But quite recently, it looked as though Mr Strong might have met his match.

One day, Mr Strong met Little Miss Tiny on his way home from the shops. Little Miss Tiny was crying.

"What ever is the matter?" asked Mr Strong.

Little Miss Tiny told him. She had been walking back to her house, carrying a lollipop over her shoulder when a huge, ugly Ogre had leapt out from behind a bush blocking her path.

"Gimme yer lollipop!"

the Ogre had demanded.

Poor Little Miss Tiny had no choice, but to give the Ogre her lollipop. Mr Strong was appalled.

"It is not far to my house," he said. "I'll make you a cup of tea and we can work out what is to be done."

With Little Miss Tiny sitting on his shoulder, Mr Strong continued on his way.

Just around the corner, they came upon Mr Rush sitting at the side of the road, looking very shaken.

"What ever is wrong?" asked Mr Strong.

Mr Rush explained. He had been driving along the road when an **enormous,** brute of an Ogre had loomed up in the middle of the lane.

"Gimme yer car!" the Ogre had demanded.

Poor Mr Rush had no choice but to hand over his car and watch helplessly as the Ogre drove away in it.

Mr Strong suggested that Mr Rush join him and Little Miss Tiny for tea.

They had walked the last half a mile to Mr Strong's house when they met a very upset and indignant Mr Uppity.

This time Mr Strong had a very good idea what the matter was.

Mr Uppity had been on his way to the bank to count his money when a huge, horrible Ogre had stepped out from behind a tree forcing Mr Uppity to stop.

"Gimme yer hat!" the Ogre had roared.

Poor Mr Uppity had no choice but to give the Ogre his hat. Which, not surprisingly, was far too small for the Ogre.

"I've heard enough!" announced Mr Strong. "Go inside and make yourselves some tea. I'm off to find this Ogre. I shan't be long."

Mr Strong had a pretty good idea where he might find the Ogre. Behind his garden, on the other side of the hill, there was a cave in the woods. Sure enough, this was where Mr Strong found the Ogre, lounging in the entrance to the cave, eating Little Miss Tiny's lollipop.

The only trouble was, there was not one Ogre, but three! They were brothers.

The Ogres slowly raised themselves to their full, menacing height. Undaunted, Mr Strong marched up to the Ogres and introduced himself.

"Strong! Yer don't know the meaning of strong. Just look at yer!" mocked the biggest Ogre.

"If I prove I am stronger than the three of you, will you apologise to my friends and promise to stop bullying?" asked Mr Strong.

"Stronger than the three of us!"

boomed the biggest Ogre. "Even my little brother is stronger than you!"

"Can he lift this?" asked Mr Strong, raising a large rock above his head.

"Easy peasy," said the smallest Ogre.

Mr Strong passed the largest rock to the smallest Ogre, but it was too heavy for him and the Ogre dropped it on his toe.

"OWWW!" he bellowed in pain.

"Out of the way, titch,"

snarled the middle Ogre, pushing the youngest Ogre out of his way.

"I bet yer too weak to pick that up," he taunted, pointing at a huge slab of stone.

Mr Strong smiled and lifted it effortlessly.

"Your turn," said Mr Strong.

The middle Ogre tried with all his might to lift the slab of stone. He raised one end three inches off the ground before he dropped it, trapping his fingers underneath.

"OWWW!" roared the middle Ogre in pain.

"Let me 'ave a go!" thundered the third Ogre, who was possibly the least clever of the three, but by far the largest.

With an enormous effort, the biggest Ogre lifted the stone slab above his head.

"Beat that," he grunted through gritted teeth.

But then his knees began to **wobble,** his legs started to **tremble,** his arms **buckled** and the rock came down on his head, knocking him out cold!

Mr Strong picked up the biggest Ogre as if he weighed no more than a feather and carried him, with the other two brothers following behind, over the hill, back to his house where he set him down in front of his three friends.

"Now we have got all that nonsense out of the way," said Mr Strong, "I think it is time you said sorry."

"We're sorry," mumbled the three Ogres in unison.

"We can't hear you," said Mr Strong.

"We're very sorry," said the Ogre brothers more clearly.

"Now that's done we can all have some tea," announced Mr Strong.

Which they did.

Although the Ogres did not stay long, as tea parties are not really their thing.

LITTLE MISS STUBBORN
AND THE UNICORN

Little Miss Stubborn is, as you might imagine, the most stubborn person in the World.

She is as stubborn as a mule.

She is as stubborn as a herd of mules.

Once she has made her mind up about something, then there is **no** changing it.

For example, last week she decided to go on a picnic.

The weather forecast said it was going to rain.

All her friends said it was going to rain.

It was raining when she set off for her picnic.

And it rained on her picnic.

But she is so stubborn, she did not even take an umbrella with her.

The day after her soggy picnic, a very excited Little Miss Chatterbox telephoned.

"You'll never guess who I spoke to this morning," exclaimed Little Miss Chatterbox. "I was walking through the wood, the one down by the river, when I saw the most extraordinary sight! You'll never guess what it was. It was so exciting! I hardly know how to tell you. You just won't believe it, but it's true. I saw it with my own two eyes. It was incredible. **I met a Unicorn!"**

MR. MEN MAGICAL TREASURY

Little Miss Chatterbox can take rather a long time to say what she wants to say.

"Nonsense!" snorted Little Miss Stubborn. "Unicorns don't exist."

"But ..." began Little Miss Chatterbox.

"I don't believe you," interrupted Little Miss Stubborn and she hung up.

The next day, Little Miss Stubborn met Mr Bump.

A very excited Mr Bump.

"You'll never guess what I bumped into this morning. **I bumped into a Unicorn!"** he announced, proudly.

"**Nonsense,**" snapped Little Miss Stubborn. "Unicorns don't exist!"

"**But …**" began Mr Bump.

"**But nothing. I don't believe you,**" said Little Miss Stubborn and she walked away.

She passed by Little Miss Sunshine who was in her garden.

"If only you had been here half an hour earlier," called Little Miss Sunshine. "There was a Unicorn here in my garden and I rode on its back!"

"**Nonsense!**" exclaimed Little Miss Stubborn. "Unicorns don't exist!"

"**But …**" began Little Miss Sunshine.

"No buts, **I don't believe you!"** interrupted Little Miss Stubborn.

And so it carried on.

It seemed that **everyone** had seen a Unicorn.

Mr Tickle had tickled a Unicorn.

Little Miss Greedy had fed a Unicorn.

And Mr Muddle declared that he had seen a unicycle.

Although, of course he meant to say a Unicorn.

And would Little Miss Stubborn believe any of her friends?

Of course not!

Not for a moment.

Little Miss Stubborn turned down the lane, through a gate into her garden.

And there, clear as day, helping itself to an apple from her apple tree, was a Unicorn.

"Hello," said the Unicorn. "I have been told that you do not believe in Unicorns."

"That's right," said Little Miss Stubborn. **"Unicorns do not exist."**

"So what am I?" asked the Unicorn.

"You," said Little Miss Stubborn, walking up to the Unicorn, "are **a horse!"**

With which, Little Miss Stubborn reached up and grabbed the horn on the Unicorn's head.

But to Little Miss Stubborn's great surprise, the horn was real.

The Unicorn really was a Unicorn.

"Well?" said the Unicorn. "What do you have to say now?"

Little Miss Stubborn screwed up her face and crossed her arms.

"I don't believe in Unicorns!" she said, and stamped her foot.

Stubborn to the very end.

MR. NOSEY
AND THE
BEANSTALK

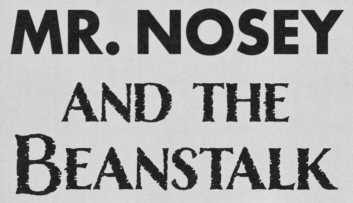

Mr Nosey is one of those people who is curious about everything.

If he comes across a parcel he will start to wonder what's inside it.

And the more **curious** he becomes the more he has to know.

And even if it is addressed to someone else, Mr Nosey will not be able to stop himself opening it.

Just to have a look.

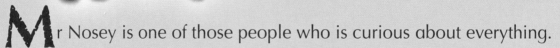

His curiosity always gets the better of him.

One day, Mr Nosey was out for a walk when he met a **Wizard.**

The Wizard was holding a small bag.

Mr Nosey, being Mr Nosey, had to know what was inside the bag.

The Wizard told him that it was a bag full of **magic beans.**

Mr Nosey had to know what was magic about them.

"I will give you one bean," said the Wizard. "And if you take it home and plant it, you will find out. That is, if you're sure that you want to find out."

What a silly question. Of course Mr Nosey was sure he wanted to find out!

At home, Mr Nosey planted the bean in his garden.

The next morning he could not believe his eyes.

There in the middle of his garden was a **giant beanstalk** that stretched up into the clouds.

As Mr Nosey admired the beanstalk, a thought occurred to him.

"What could be at the top of the beanstalk?"

The more he thought this thought, the more curious he became, and the more curious he became, the more he had to know.

So he began to climb the beanstalk.

He climbed …

… and he climbed …

… and he climbed.

Right up into the clouds.

And when he reached the top he could not believe his eyes. (For the second time that day.)

There in the clouds was a **giant castle!**

And then a thought occurred to him.

"Who might live in a castle in the clouds?"

And the thought grew into curiosity, and the curiosity got the better of him. So he set out across the clouds to the castle.

The **giant castle** had a **giant door**, and in the **giant door** there was a **giant keyhole.**

Mr Nosey cannot pass a keyhole and resist the urge to have a peek, and this time was no different.

Except that this time it was different because Mr Nosey could fit through the keyhole.

Once inside, it quickly became apparent that the **'who'** who lived in the castle was a **giant.**

Now you or I would have sensibly left as fast as we could.

In fact, we would not have been there in the first place. But Mr Nosey, as you can guess, could not resist having a look around.

Mr Nosey went into the Giant's kitchen and in the corner were three small cupboards. Of course Mr Nosey had to know what was inside them.

He opened the first cupboard. Inside was a small bag.

Before he could look inside the bag he heard a terrifying sound.

THUMP!

THUMP!

THUMP!

It was the thud of the Giant's heavy-booted footsteps, somewhere in the castle, and they were getting closer.

Mr Nosey grabbed the bag, scrambled through the keyhole and slithered back down the beanstalk as fast as he could.

Safely back at home he discovered that the bag was full of gold coins!

That night he could not sleep. He lay in bed thinking about the other two cupboards.

"What could they contain?"

He just had to know.

Early the next morning, back up the beanstalk went Mr Nosey, back through the keyhole and back to the second cupboard in the Giant's kitchen.

Inside it was a hen.

"That's curious," thought Mr Nosey to himself, not for the first time in this story!

He picked up the hen and there was a **golden egg.**

"A hen that lays golden eggs," murmured Mr Nosey. "I'll need to take this home for a closer look."

Just then, Mr Nosey heard the heavy boots of the Giant coming down the stairs.

THUMP!

THUMP!

THUMP!

Mr Nosey tucked the hen under his arm and ran for his life.

The hen fascinated Mr Nosey, but it did not stop him thinking about the third cupboard.

He was terrified of the Giant, but his curiosity overcame his fear and so, the following morning, back to the Giant's kitchen he went.

He opened the third cupboard and in it was a **golden harp.**

A golden harp that was singing!

Mr Nosey sat and listened to the harp. He felt safe, knowing that he would be able to hear the Giant's loud boots coming.

But the Giant was wearing his slippers that morning, which is how he caught Mr Nosey.

"So you're the thief!" boomed the Giant. "I have a mind to grind your bones to make my bread!"

Mr Nosey's eyes nearly popped out of his head.

"But I won't," continued the Giant. "I prefer cornflakes for breakfast. Now, I know what to do with you. Since you are so interested in what is in my cupboards, you can clean them out for me."

And Mr Nosey did.

It took him three whole days.

Giants' cupboards are … well, **giant.**

"Now let that be a lesson to you," said the Giant.

And you'd think it would have been, but the very next day Mr Nosey came upon an empty house and the front door was open and on the kitchen table were three bowls of porridge …

… but that's **another story.**

LITTLE MISS SHY
AND THE FAIRY
GODMOTHER

Little Miss Shy is the shyest person that you will ever meet.

Except that you will probably never meet her because she never goes out.

So she didn't get excited when she received an invitation to Little Miss Splendid's Grand Ball. She got worried and flustered.

She wanted to go. But she worried about all the people. So, she would not go. But she wanted to go.

Little Miss Shy was in a dilemma.

Plucking up all her courage, she rang Little Miss Sunshine for some advice.

"Do you know what I would do?" said Little Miss Sunshine. "I'd go out and buy a new pair of shoes. It always gives my confidence a boost!"

So Little Miss Shy followed her advice and went to the shoe shop.

"Please, I'd like to buy some new shoes," said Little Miss Shy in a very quiet voice.

"I CAN'T HEAR YOU!" boomed Little Miss Bossy, who worked in the shoe shop. **"SPEAK UP!"**

Little Miss Shy blushed.

"Oooh, look!" cried Little Miss Naughty. "She's turning **pink!**"

"Good gosh, you're right!" exclaimed Little Miss Bossy.

105

And she was right. Little Miss Shy was turning **pinker** and **pinker.**

"She looks like a strawberry blancmange!" giggled Little Miss Naughty, cruelly.

Little Miss Shy was, by this stage, pink from the top of her head to the tips of her toes. She burst into tears and ran out of the shop.

Poor Little Miss Shy.

She was so **miserable** she could not sleep.

She sat in front of the fire quietly crying to herself. "I will never go to the Ball," she sobbed.

"Oh yes you will," came a faraway reply.

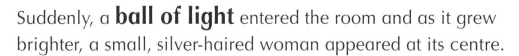

Suddenly, a **ball of light** entered the room and as it grew brighter, a small, silver-haired woman appeared at its centre.

"Who are you?" asked Little Miss Shy.

"I am your **Fairy Godmother,"** said the woman, kindly. "And you will go to the Ball."

"But I'm too shy," said Little Miss Shy.

"Not with the right pair of shoes," said the Fairy Godmother, who waved her **magic wand.**

Little Miss Shy's old bedroom slippers transformed into a pair of **glass ballroom slippers.**

The **most beautiful** shoes Little Miss Shy had ever set eyes on.

Then, the most **amazing** thing happened.

Little Miss Shy was suddenly filled with confidence. **All her shyness disappeared!**

"But, you must remember," warned the Fairy Godmother, "that on the last stroke of **midnight** on the night of the Ball, if you are still wearing the shoes, they will turn back into ordinary bedroom slippers."

The following evening, Little Miss Shy went to the Ball and she had the most wonderful evening of her life.

She **danced** all night long.

Everyone was **dazzled** by her beautiful glass slippers.

Little Miss Shy was so unlike her usual self that **nobody** recognised her.

Near the end of the Ball, Little Miss Splendid stood up and made an **announcement.**

"I have a surprise for you all. There is a prize for the **best dancer** at the Ball tonight, and I and my fellow judges have decided that this prize should be awarded to ... " she paused, **"... the girl in the glass ballroom slippers!"**

As Little Miss Splendid spoke, **the bell** in the clock tower **rang** the first stroke of **midnight.**

In a flash, Little Miss Shy remembered the Fairy Godmother's warning.

She couldn't go up and receive her prize without the glass slippers. Little Miss Shy could feel herself starting to blush. She **panicked** and **fled** from the ballroom.

As she ran, one of the glass slippers fell from her foot.

"Where is the girl in the glass ballroom slippers?" called Little Miss Splendid.

But nobody could find her.

She had disappeared.

All they could find was one glass slipper.

"I must have my winner!" cried Little Miss Splendid. "Search the land until you find her!"

So Little Miss Splendid's friends went out in search of a girl whose foot would fit the glass slipper. Everybody wanted to claim the prize, **but nobody's foot would fit.**

Little Miss Bossy and Little Miss Naughty tried on the slipper and of course it did not fit either of them.

"You should try Little Miss Shy," suggested Little Miss Naughty, slyly.

"Let's go and watch her turn pink," she said to Little Miss Bossy.

"Oooh, you are naughty," giggled Little Miss Bossy.

So they all arrived at Little Miss Shy's house.

Poor Little Miss Shy. She did not know where to put herself.

And of course, **she turned pink.**

But not as pink as Little Miss Naughty and Little Miss Bossy when the glass slipper fitted Little Miss Shy's foot!

They were speechless!

"Little Miss Splendid will want to present your prize to you in person," said Mr Happy.

Little Miss Shy's prize was a pair of pink dancing shoes.

Her Fairy Godmother smiled down on her as Little Miss Splendid put the shoes on Little Miss Shy's feet.

They fitted perfectly.

And they matched Little Miss Shy perfectly.

Little Miss Shy was **very proud** and **very pink!**

MR. GREEDY
AND THE
GINGERBEAD MAN

It was not long after he'd finished his breakfast that Mr Greedy started to feel hungry again.

He had eaten **3** packets of cornflakes, **2** loaves of bread and **1** pot of jam, but Mr Greedy's tummy was telling him that it was feeling peckish.

"What to have?" thought Mr Greedy to himself.

"I know," he said out loud. "I shall make a **gingerbread man."**

And because he is Mr Greedy, he made an **extra large** gingerbread man, which he put in the oven.

And while he was waiting for it to bake, he had a snack.

A chocolate biscuit.

Followed by two more chocolate biscuits.

In fact a whole packet of chocolate biscuits.

And as he finished the last biscuit, he heard a **knocking** sound.

It was coming from the oven.

"How odd," he thought to himself and he opened the oven door. And to his great surprise, out jumped his gingerbread man who ran round the kitchen crying:

"Run, run as fast as you can!
You can't catch me,
I'm the Gingerbread Man!"

The Gingerbread Man ran out of the door and down the garden path.

Mr Greedy gave chase, but the Gingerbread Man was right. Mr Greedy couldn't catch him, and the Gingerbread Man was soon out of sight.

The Gingerbread Man ran up a hill and at the top he passed Mr Bump fetching water from a well.

"Run, run as fast as you can! You can't catch me, I'm the Gingerbread Man!"

Mr Bump gave chase, but …

Oops!

Mr Bump tripped over his pail of water and rolled all the way down the hill and bumped his head.

The Gingerbread Man ran on.

He ran past Mr Lazy, asleep in his hammock.

*"Run, run as fast as you can!
You can't catch me,
I'm the Gingerbread Man!"*

Mr Lazy opened an eye.

"You're not wrong," he said and he went back to sleep.

On ran the Gingerbread Man.

He ran past Little Miss Late.

*"Run, run as fast as you can!
You can't catch me,
I'm the Gingerbread Man!"*

Little Miss Late took up the chase, but the Gingerbread Man was too fast.

"Oh dear. I can't even catch a bus, let alone the Gingerbread Man," sighed Little Miss Late.

Nobody could catch the
Gingerbread Man.

Mr Slow was too slow.

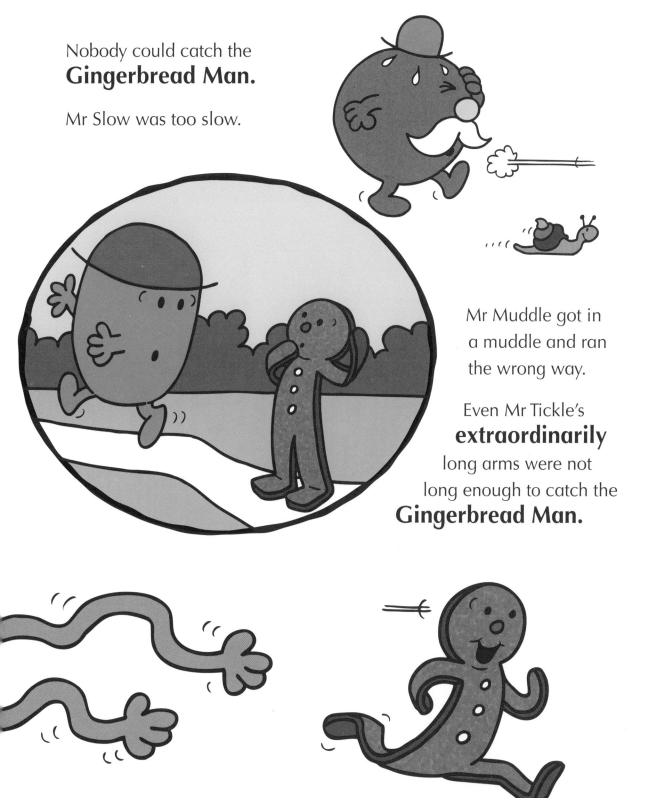

Mr Muddle got in
a muddle and ran
the wrong way.

Even Mr Tickle's
extraordinarily
long arms were not
long enough to catch the
Gingerbread Man.

"**Nobody can catch me,**" boasted the Gingerbread Man, and he was so pleased with himself that he decided to lie down for a rest.

And he fell fast asleep.

"**Caught you,**" said a voice, and a big pink hand picked up the Gingerbread Man.

"Slow and steady wins the race," continued Mr Greedy.

Mr Greedy took a big bite of the Gingerbread Man.

"**Oh dear!**" cried the Gingerbread Man. "I'm a quarter gone!"

Mr Greedy took another bite.

"Oh dear! Now I'm half gone!"

And another bite.

"Oh dear! I'm three quarters gone!"

And then one last bite.

"Oh dear," said Mr Greedy. "Now it's all gone …"

"… and I'm still hungry!"

THE THREE LITTLE MISSES
AND THE BIG BAD WOLF

Little Miss Naughty had decided to build a new house for herself. But because she did not know how to build a house, she asked her good friend Mr Silly to build it for her.

And he did.

He made it with **straw.**

A house built of **straw?**

How silly!

But it was not just silly, it was also dangerous because not long after Little Miss Naughty had moved in, the Big Bad Wolf came calling.

He knocked on Little Miss Naughty's straw door.

"Little Miss," called the wolf. "It's the **Big Bad Wolf.** Won't you let me come in?"

"Not on your Nellie," replied Little Miss Naughty, cheekily. **"I won't let you in."**

"Then I'll **huff** and I'll **puff** and I'll **blow your house down,"** cried the wolf.

And he did, because that is the sort of thing that Big Bad Wolves get up to.

But Little Miss Naughty had had a lot of practice at jumping out of windows, the naughty girl!

She leaped out of the back window and ran all the way through the woods to the house of her friend, Little Miss Trouble.

Now, as it so happened, Little Miss Trouble had also just had a house built for herself.

A house built by Mr Mean.

And as you probably know Mr Mean does not like to spend money, so he had built Little Miss Trouble's house as cheaply as he could.

He had built it with **sticks.**

A house built of **sticks?**

How mean!

Shortly after Little Miss Naughty arrived, the wolf, who had followed her, knocked on the door.

"Little Miss and Little Miss, it's the **Big Bad Wolf.** Won't you let me come in?"

"Not on your Nellie! **We will not let you in!**" they replied.

"Then I'll **huff** and I'll **puff** and I'll **blow your house down!**" cried the wolf.

And he did.

So the two Little Misses ran out of the back door and stole Mr Funny's car.

I know! How naughty!

They raced off to Little Miss Bad's house with the wolf

chasing

after

them.

Little Miss Bad had employed a proper builder to build her house.

Mr Brick.

Brick by name and **brick** by nature.

So, of course, he had made Little Miss Bad's house out of **bricks.**

Not long after the two Little Misses burst into Little Miss Bad's house, there was a knock at the door.

"That will be the Big Bad Wolf," said Little Miss Naughty.

"This is the Big Bad Wolf ..." began the wolf.

"We know!" chorused the three Little Misses.

"Little Miss, Little Miss and Little Miss, won't you let me come in?" asked the wolf.

"Not on your Nellie! **We won't let you come in!"** cried the three Little Misses.

"Then I'll **huff** and I'll **puff** and I'll **blow your house down!"** roared the wolf.

And he did. Or, at least he huffed and puffed, but Little Miss Bad's brick house did not fall down.

It was too strong.

"Bother," said the wolf.

And then he had another idea.

"Little Miss, Little Miss and Little Miss, I know of a lovely orchard on a hill on Mr Field's farm. Will you meet me there tomorrow morning at seven o'clock? We can have **apples** for breakfast?"

The three Little Misses agreed.

They had a plan.

The three Little Misses were not just naughty, trouble and bad, they were also clever. The next day, they got up at six o'clock to get to the orchard ahead of the Wolf and set a trap for him.

But the Wolf, who was even more clever, had arrived even earlier.

"Got you!" he cried, leaping out from his hiding place behind an apple tree.

At first, the three Little Misses were frightened.

And then Little Miss Naughty had a thought.

For the first time in their lives they could be naughty, troublesome and bad and they would be in the right!

"You might be **Big** and you might be **Bad,"** said Little Miss Naughty, "but **I am Naughty."**

"And I am Trouble," said Little Miss Trouble.

"And I am Bad!" said Little Miss Bad.

"And we'll **huff** and we'll **puff** and **we'll blow you down!"** cried the three Little Misses all together.

And they did.

They huffed and they puffed and they blew the Big Bad Wolf all the way down the hill.

The Wolf **rolled** and **bounced** and **bumped** so much you might almost have felt sorry for him.

But not quite.

LITTLE MISS CHATTERBOX
AND THE FROG PRINCE

I t will come as no surprise to you to hear that Little Miss Chatterbox likes to chatter. She will chatter all day long. Non stop, incessantly, without a pause, until the cows come home …

… go to bed …

… and wake up the next morning.

And it will also come as no surprise to you to hear that all this **chattering** gets on people's nerves. Particularly some people. People like Little Miss Bossy, who got cornered by Little Miss Chatterbox outside the post office.

"Good morning, Little Miss Bossy," started Little Miss Chatterbox. "Although good is probably not really the right description with all this rain we've been having and actually we're getting **wet** standing around chatting in the **rain** like this but it was so nice to see you that I thought I must stop and say 'Good morning' although as I just said good is not really …"

"Oh, do be quiet!" cried Little Miss Bossy, and she stomped off down the street.

And impatient people like Mr Rude, who got caught behind Little Miss Chatterbox in a queue at the butcher's.

"I must say Mr Chop that this is a wonderful display of meat," she said to the butcher. "It must take you a very long time to prepare it all. What time do you get up in the morning?

It must be very early. I get up quite early but you must get up even earlier. I bet you have sausages in the morning for breakfast. I have a bowl of…"

"Who cares!" shouted Mr Rude and he stormed out of the shop.

Poor Little Miss Chatterbox.

It is not very nice to be shouted at just when you think you are enjoying a polite conversation with somebody.

Sometimes it makes Little Miss Chatterbox feel very sad, and one of those times she went for a walk in the woods.

As she walked along, talking to herself, she came to a pond where she saw a **frog** sitting on a lily pad, so she sat down for a rest.

"Well, Mr Frog, you have a lovely spot here in the sun. It must be nice being a frog and not having everybody tell you to be quiet," she said to the frog. "Nobody else wants to listen to me so I might as well **talk to you."**

And so she did.

She talked for hours to the frog.

She poured her heart out.

Poor Little Miss Chatterbox.

And all the while, the frog sat very still on his lily pad, watching her.

Finally, Little Miss Chatterbox paused for a breath.

"Well, that's a terribly sad tale," said the frog.

Said the frog!

The frog could speak!

Little Miss Chatterbox could not believe her ears.

"Well I never," said Little Miss Chatterbox. "A talking frog."

The frog beamed. "It's good to have someone so interesting to talk to," he said.

The frog and Little Miss Chatterbox had a wonderful conversation. They talked about everything and anything until it was time for Little Miss Chatterbox to go home.

"Could I come back tomorrow?" asked Little Miss Chatterbox.

"That would be lovely," replied the frog.

And she did go back the next day.

And the day after that.

And even the day after that.

In fact, she went back **every day** for the next week.

Then one day, Little Miss Chatterbox said, "You are such a good listener, **I could kiss you."**

And without saying another word, she did.

She kissed the frog!

And then something utterly remarkable happened.

With a clap of **thunder** and in a cloud of **smoke,** the frog magically turned into a **prince.**

For the first time in her life, Little Miss Chatterbox was lost for words.

"Thank you!" cried the prince. "A bad wizard turned me into a frog when I was young because I wouldn't stop talking and only a freely-given kiss could break the **spell!"**

The prince then took Little Miss Chatterbox to his kingdom, where everybody welcomed him back with open arms.

And the prince was so **grateful** that he gave Little Miss Chatterbox a job at the palace.

She is now the **Official Royal Chatterer** on the palace radio station!

MR. FUNNY
AND THE
MAGIC LAMP

Mr Funny lives in a teapot.

A teapot house.

How ridiculous I hear you say, but it suited Mr Funny right down to its spout.

Now, one day last spring, Mr Funny discovered an old trunk in his attic, which is under the lid.

And in the trunk he found a carpet.

A carpet that gave him a surprise.

For it was a magic carpet.
A magic flying carpet.

Mr Funny was very excited.

There and then he decided
to go on a trip to see where the
magic carpet would take him.

So on that spring morning he set off on an **adventure.**

Mr Funny flew over Lazyland, where he woke up Mr Lazy with a very
loud raspberry and a funny face.

Mr Lazy laughed so much he fell out of bed.

Mr Funny and his magic carpet flew over Fatland, where Mr Funny made Mr Skinny laugh.

He laughed so much he tripped over a daisy and dropped the breadcrumb he was carrying for his picnic lunch.

And they flew over Coldland, where Mr Funny made Mr Sneeze laugh.

He laughed so much that he stopped sneezing!

The magic carpet **flew on and on.**

They flew over mountains and valleys and over the sea.

Finally, they arrived in a **desert.**

But there was nobody there. Nobody to laugh at Mr Funny's funny faces.

Then, just as he was about to leave, Mr Funny saw something half buried in the sand. **It was a lamp.**

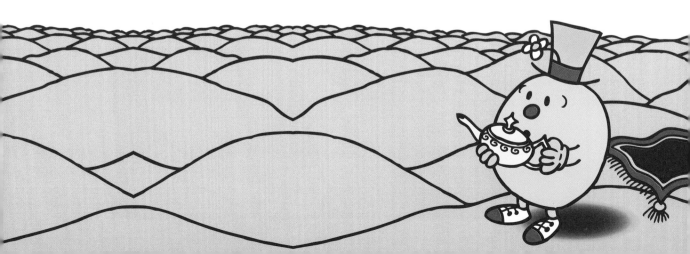

"What a grubby old lamp," he said to himself and he gave it a rub.

Suddenly, with a clap of **thunder** and in a cloud of **smoke,** a **genie** appeared in front of Mr Funny.

Which was all very exciting, but what Mr Funny noticed most of all was how miserable the genie looked.

Mr Funny had never seen anyone look so **unhappy.**

"Master," said the genie, glumly, "I am the Genie of the Lamp and I appear before you to grant you **three wishes."**

To the genie's surprise, Mr Funny pulled one of his famous funny faces.

But the genie did not laugh.

He did not chuckle.

He did not even smile.

Not a flicker.

"Oh dear," said Mr Funny. It was going to take a bit more than a funny face to **cheer up** this genie.

And then he had a thought.

"For my first wish, **I wish** for a piano-playing elephant."

"As you command, Master," said the genie, and then before you could say 'broken piano stool' a piano-playing elephant appeared before them.

Mr Funny roared with laughter.

It was hilarious!

But it was not funny enough to make the genie laugh.

He looked just as glum as before.

Mr Funny had another thought.

"For my second wish, **I wish** for a mouse."

And before you could say 'squeak' a mouse appeared.

And as Mr Funny and you probably know, great big elephants are frightened of teeny tiny mice.

The elephant **trumpeted** in fear and jumped on top of the piano, which broke under the elephant's weight.

Mr Funny laughed with delight.

"Now, that was **funny,**" chuckled Mr Funny.

"Not really," said the genie, who looked just as unhappy as before.

"You are a gloomy fellow," said Mr Funny.

"You would be too," said the genie, "if you had to live in that lamp!"

"It must be a **tight** admitted Mr Funny.

"You can say that again," grumbled the genie. "There's no room even to cough living in a lamp."

"I live in a teapot. A very comfortable teapot, mind you," said Mr Funny, and then yet another thought struck him.

"For my third wish, **I wish** your lamp was a house."

And before you could say 'bring me a builder' the Genie's lamp had turned into a **house!**

The genie smiled.

Only a flicker of a smile, but at least a smile.

"That's more like it," said Mr Funny.
"Now, how am I going to get this elephant back home?
I know! **I wish ...**"

"I'm sorry," interrupted the genie. "You've used up your three wishes."

So Mr Funny and the elephant had to squeeze onto the magic carpet for their ride home. It was quite a sight.

Rather funny, in fact.

So funny, the **Genie roared with laughter!**

LITTLE MISS SUNSHINE
AND THE THREE
BEARS

Little Miss Sunshine went for a walk in the woods.

And because it was a lovely hot day
she decided to go for a long walk.

She walked.

And she walked ...

... and she walked.

And then, suddenly, the weather turned for the worse. A storm arrived with a great **crash** and **boom** of thunder.

She ran through the woods looking for shelter from the rain, which she found in the form of a cottage in a clearing in the woods.

She knocked at the door.

"Come in!" said a very loud, gruff voice.

The door led onto a kitchen and sitting around the table were three bears.

A **big** bear, a **medium** bear and a **little** bear.

On the table were three bowls of porridge.

A **big** bowl, a **medium** bowl and a **little** bowl.

"We're just going out for a walk while our porridge cools down," said the middle bear.

"You can stay here if you keep an eye on our porridge and make sure no one eats it."

"Thank you, I will," agreed Little Miss Sunshine, and the three bears left.

Bears do not mind the rain.

Little Miss Sunshine settled down to wait, glad to be out of the storm.

Suddenly the door burst open and Mr Greedy barged his way in.

"Mr Greedy, what are you…" began Little Miss Sunshine, but before she could finish Mr Greedy spied the three bowls on the table.

"Ooh, Porridge!" he cried. "I'm starving!"

"You can't eat that porridge!" cried Little Miss Sunshine.

But Mr Greedy was hungry and he didn't listen.

The first **big** bowl he tried was **too hot.**

The next **medium** bowl was **too cold.**

But the last **small** bowl was **just right.**

So right that before Little Miss Sunshine knew it, Mr Greedy had **finished it all.**

Mr Greedy looked at the small empty bowl.

"Well, that wasn't nearly enough for me," he said. "I'm off to find a **bigger** meal," and he left as suddenly as he had arrived.

Mr Greedy had hardly been gone a minute when the door was flung open for a second time and in stumbled Mr Clumsy.

"Hello, Mr Clumsy," said Little Miss Sunshine. "What brings you here?"

"Oooh, my poor feet!" he moaned. "I've been walking for miles. I need a rest." And he went into the living room where there were three chairs.

"You can't come in here!" cried Little Miss Sunshine.

But Mr Clumsy didn't listen and he sat in the **big** chair.

It was **too lumpy.**

147

The **medium** chair was **too soft.**

But the **small** chair… well, the **small** chair was **just right.**

So right that Mr Clumsy leaned back, but being his usual clumsy self, he leaned back too far and with a loud **CRACK!** the chair broke.

Mr Clumsy jumped up and said that he had just remembered something he had to do very urgently.

And he left.

Poor Little Miss Sunshine.

She looked miserably at the broken chair.

What was she going to say to the three bears?

It was then that Little Miss Sunshine heard a **loud,** gruff voice coming from the kitchen.

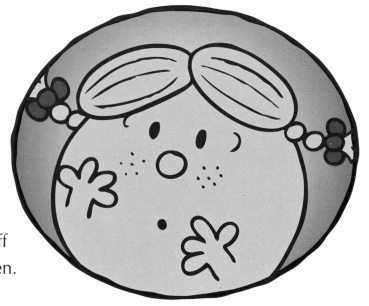

"Who's been eating **my** porridge?" demanded the voice.

"Who's been eating **my** porridge?" asked the medium voice.

And then a tiny, squeaky voice said, "Who's been eating **my** porridge and eaten it all up?"

Then the three bears came into the living room.

"Who's been sitting in **my** chair?" said the big bear.

"Who's been sitting in **my** chair?" said the medium bear.

"And who's been sitting in **my** chair and broken it?" cried the little bear.

The three bears glared angrily at Little Miss Sunshine.

"Not me!" she cried.

149

Just then the door flew open for a third time. It was Mr Lazy.

"Aaargh," he yawned. "It's time for my nap! I need a bed!"

"You're not sleeping in **my** bed!" boomed the big bear.

"You're not sleeping in **my** bed!" said the medium bear.

"And you're not sleeping in **my** bed!" squeaked the little bear.

Mr Lazy's face fell.

"You can come and sleep at **my** house," said Little Miss Sunshine.

The bears were very happy to hear this, so Mr Lazy and Little Miss Sunshine said **goodbye** and set off back to her house.

However, as you know, it was a very long walk and Mr Lazy kept having to stop for a quick forty winks so it was very late when they finally arrived.

Late enough for it to be Little Miss Sunshine's bedtime too.

In fact it was everyone's bedtime.

Big bear was in his big bed.

Medium bear was in his medium bed.

Little bear was in his little bed.

Mr Lazy was tucked up in Little Miss Sunshine's bed.

And Little Miss Sunshine was …

… on the sofa!

Poor Little Miss Sunshine.

LITTLE MISS PRINCESS
AND THE PEA

Late one night last week, on her way home Little Miss Princess got caught in a terrible storm and her coach got stuck in the mud.

She saw a light in the distance and decided to seek help and a bed for the night.

She walked through the wind and rain and lightning to the house.

On the way she lost her **crown.**

Little Miss Princess arrived at the huge house **exhausted** and looking very **wet** and bedraggled.

In fact **not** looking like a **Princess** at all.

She knocked on the tall front doors.

It was Mr Uppity's house. Mr Uppity is the richest man in the World. He is also one of the rudest men in the World.

"What do you want?" he demanded, rudely, when he opened the door.

Little Miss Princess explained what had happened and asked for a bed for the night.

"You're not coming in here!" he bellowed. **"You'll ruin my expensive rugs!"**

"Please can you help me," begged Little Miss Princess. "I'm so cold and tired and I just need a bed for the night."

"Go round to the back and I'll see what I can do," he said crossly. With which he slammed the door in her face.

What a rude man!

Poor Little Miss Princess had to trudge all the way round the house. Mr Uppity opened the back door.

"Took your time! You can sleep in there," he said, pointing to a cold, damp cellar.

"But I'm a Princess!" spluttered Little Miss Princess.

"You don't look like one!" snapped Mr Uppity. "You don't even have a crown."

"I lost it in the storm," explained Little Miss Princess.

"A likely story," said Mr Uppity. "If you are a Princess then you will have to **prove it!"**

Mr Uppity led Little Miss Princess into his enormous dining room. The dining table was vast and seated round it were some guests.

Mr Uppity explained the situation to his guests and asked for their suggestions.

"Princesses are really good at dancing. **Let's dance!"** suggested Mr Bump.

And of course Mr Bump trod on her toes and sent her flying across the floor.

"Hopeless!" cried Mr Uppity. "Can't dance, so she can't possibly be a Princess!"

"Princesses are really good at **waving,"** said Mr Tickle.

Now, Little Miss Princess was very proud of her waving and loved to wave to people from her coach, but every time she raised her arm Mr Tickle **tickled** her.

He tickled her so much she fell over on the floor.

"Can't wave, can't dance and look at her, on the floor again!" said Mr Uppity, impatiently. "Decidedly **not a Princess!"**

"I have heard," piped up Little Miss Splendid, "that Princesses are very delicate. So delicate that if they sleep with even **a pea** under their mattress they will wake in the morning bruised all over."

"Mmmm," said Mr Uppity. "That's an **interesting idea."**

So Mr Uppity went off to find a pea and the others all trooped upstairs.

Mr Mean lifted the mattress and Mr Uppity placed the pea underneath.

Mr Mean looked at the bed. "Not much of a test," he said.

"Quite right, Mr Mean. **More mattresses!"** he ordered.

So they piled mattress after mattress, one on top of the other, until they nearly reached the ceiling.

And then Little Miss Princess climbed on top.

"Good night," said Mr Uppity, and he turned out the light.

And then Mr Uppity went to bed.

Although not the sort of bed he had hoped for.

There was not a bed in the house left with a mattress on it.

Mr Uppity was up very early the next day. Partly to see how the test had worked, but also because he had had a dreadful night's sleep.

"How did you sleep?" Mr Uppity asked Little Miss Princess.

"I had a wonderful night's sleep," she replied.

"Ah!" cried Mr Uppity. "I knew you weren't a Princess!"

"And yet, I still got to sleep in your biggest and most comfortable bed!" beamed Little Miss Princess.

"Oh," said a suddenly crestfallen Mr Uppity.

"And if you are going to test for Princesses in the future," she added, "you should use an uncooked pea, not a cooked one."

With which she lifted the mattresses and revealed a **squashed pea!**

Mr Uppity went very red in the face and did not know what to say, he was so embarrassed.

And Little Miss Princess went home.

"A waste of a **good pea,** if you ask me," muttered Mr Mean.

Mr. Men Magical Treasury © 2017 THOIP (a SANRIO company)
Printed and published under licence from Price Stern Sloan, Inc., Los Angeles.
First published in Great Britain by Egmont UK Limited
The Yellow Building, 1 Nicholas Road, London W11 4AN

Mr. Happy and the Wizard first published 2004
Little Miss Sunshine and the Wicked Witch first published 2005
Mr. Tickle and the Dragon first published 2005
Little Miss Naughty and the Good Fairy first published 2003
Mr. Jelly and the Pirates first published 2006
Little Miss Trouble and the Mermaid first published 2005
Mr. Bump and the Knight first published 2007
Little Miss Splendid and the Princess first published 2010
Mr. Noisy and the Giant first published 2005
Little Miss Lucky and the Naughty Pixies first published 2007
Mr. Strong and the Ogre first published 2008
Little Miss Stubborn and the Unicorn first published 2010
Mr. Nosey and the Beanstalk first published 2009
Little Miss Shy and the Fairy Godmother first published 2009
Mr. Greedy and the Gingerbread Man first published 2013
The Three Little Misses and the Big Bad Wolf first published 2013
Little Miss Chatterbox and the Frog Prince first published 2014
Mr. Funny and the Magic Lamp first published 2014
Little Miss Sunshine and the Three Bears first published 2015
Little Miss Princess and the Pea first published 2015

ISBN 978 1 4052 8827 9
67731/1
Printed in Malaysia